Catbird's Calling

Catbird's Calling

AND OTHER ANIMAL STORIES
Compiled by the Editors
of
Highlights for Children

CONTENTS

Catbird's Calling

By Virginia L. Kroll

Miranda hears meowing in the mulberry tree. She laughs and snaps her fingers, beckoning. "Here kitty, kitty, kitty."

The meowing continues, and Miranda wonders. She crouches underneath the mulberry umbrella. It isn't Cream Puff, with her pale orange fur and stripes you can only see up close. It's a slate-gray bird with a neat black cap and a rusty tail patch.

Mrs. Wilson yells from across the fence, "Catbird's calling. Spring is here to stay."

7

"Hooray!" Miranda shouts. She and the catbird play hide-and-seek through the branches.

Cream Puff comes and curls around her ankles. Catbird screeches a last meow and flies roller-coaster fashion into Mrs. Wilson's lilacs.

Next day the sun is summer warm. "Let's have a picnic," Miranda says, and she and her brother take their lunch outside. They spread napkins on the picnic table and set down their food. They talk about summer things between bites, legs dangling beneath last year's cobwebs.

They wave to Mrs. Wilson across the yard. "Flower-planting time," she yells. Her face is hidden by leaves and stems that sprout from the flat box she is carrying.

Michael finishes first and dashes to the swings. "Bet I can still swing higher than you."

"Bet you can't." Miranda leaves her sandwich and jumps on the other swing.

"See? Told you I'm better," he says, grinning. Michael is right. He can still swing higher, no matter how hard Miranda pumps.

"You're just older," she says, straining with all her might. "I'll beat you by fall."

Suddenly Michael slows down, scraping the dirt patch with a sneaker toe. "Hey, Miranda, look. That bird is stealing your lunch."

Miranda slows down, too. "It's Catbird," she says, remembering.

Mrs. Wilson's laugh drifts over the fence. "You must have had peanut butter."

"How did you know?" Miranda asks.

"Because catbirds love peanut butter," Mrs. Wilson replies.

Miranda watches the catbird. The catbird flits and watches too and flies away with the last bit of crust.

Next day the picnic weather disappears, but Miranda throws on her raincoat and heads outside.

"Where do you think you're going?" Michael asks.

"Be right back." Her answer trickles through the closing door.

Back inside a few moments later, Miranda presses her nose to the window. She waits. And waits.

Finally, a flurry of feathers fills the window. The catbird lands on the picnic table, ruffling up against the rain and gobbling the sandwich scrap that Miranda has left it.

Miranda turns around. "Hey, Michael . . ." But he has finished his lunch long ago and is already gone from the table.

Every day Miranda leaves a small scrap of peanut butter bread on the picnic table. One day she is eating lunch at Janine's down the street when she hears Michael's voice. "Is my sister here?"

She goes to the door. "What do you want?"

"That bird is calling you, that's what," he says.

"Be right back," Miranda says to Janine. She runs home and gets some bread and spreads peanut butter on it.

The catbird is waiting on the far side of the picnic table. It doesn't fly away when she sets down the treat. Miranda watches, afraid to breathe, until her catbird has eaten every crumb.

Next day she listens for the call. She always makes sure Cream Puff is inside before she takes the bread outside. Today the catbird lands right in the middle of the table. Miranda swallows the gasp that wants to explode from her throat. She has never seen a bird this close. Its shiny, round black eyes hold her brown ones in a friendly stare. She can see the individual feathers that look like one smooth coat from far away.

She knows it can happen, and the next day she tries. When the catbird calls, she checks on Cream Puff and gets the bread and goes outside.

Miranda stands at the picnic table, crust in hand, as the catbird calls from the nearby hedge. She tries to keep her hand from trembling. She waits. And waits. She is just about to put the bread on the table when a flurry of gray feathers grazes her forehead.

For just a second, Miranda feels afraid. Then Catbird's feet light on her hand, slender toes ringing right around her fingers.

Miranda's heart pounds. Her fingertips tingle. She stands statue still until Catbird has eaten the very last crumb.

Michael tries it. So does Janine. But Catbird knows the difference.

Mrs. Wilson says over the fence, "No sense trying to change that bird's mind."

Miranda chats with Catbird then. It cocks its head at the sound of her voice and sings her wren and robin songs all summer long. It imitates grackles' squeaks and crows' squawks.

Then one day Catbird doesn't come. Miranda waits the whole day. And another. Mrs. Wilson notices. "Your friend spends winter where it's warmer," she says.

Miranda swallows hard and runs to the swing set. She starts swinging, pumping with all her might. Michael jumps on the other swing. "Bet I can still swing higher than you."

Miranda doesn't answer, but when she looks over, she sees Michael behind her, his face turning red.

Autumn spreads its gold and orange carpet on the ground, then winter whooshes in. Miranda plays board games with Michael by the fire. Cream Puff curls up in Miranda's lap, keeping them both extra snug.

One morning Miranda and Michael answer the door. It is Mrs. Wilson with a letter that the postman has delivered to her mailbox by mistake. Just before they shut the door, Michael says, "Shh. Isn't that the catbird calling you, Miranda?"

Miranda and Mrs. Wilson listen. "No," says Mrs. Wilson, pointing to the bare mulberry tree. "It's just a starling mimicking the catbird. They're good at mimicking, just like someone else we know."

Miranda squints to see the chunky black starling, feathers flecked in white.

Her eyes twinkle. "Be right back," she says.

Miranda grabs a spatula. She flings the cupboard open and twists the lid off the peanut butter jar. She checks to make sure Cream Puff is asleep on the window seat.

Miranda's heart pounds as she throws on her wool jacket and hurries into the harsh winter air. And beneath her warm mittens, she feels a tingle in her fingertips.

Chili Dog

By Anita Borgo

"Sarah, *no!* Bad dog!" shouted Mom. "Louie, stop her."

A spotted blur shot through the family room. It leaped stacks of paperback books, skidded on last night's empty pizza box, and toppled carefully sorted baseball cards. The furry fireball escaped into Louie's room and hid behind a pile of dirty laundry.

Sarah peeked from behind the hill of clothes. Her long black ears flopped back in a salute. A hot dog jutted out of her mouth like a stubby cigar.

"Give it here, girl." Louie slowly approached.

Sarah's tail wiggled, sending balled-up socks into a far corner. After a few quick bites, all that remained of Mom's lunch was a smidgen of mustard on Sarah's nose. Her tongue darted over the yellow dab and even that trace vanished.

Mom stood in the doorway. "I don't understand. If she's hungry, why doesn't she eat her dog food? Why snatch my lunch from the counter?"

"It's only a hot dog, Mom. She'll listen. She'll learn not to take food."

"She didn't understand after stealing last night's pepperoni pizza and Tuesday's Chinese food. Adopting an older dog has its problems."

Mom shoved Louie's mitt and cleats to the side and settled on the floor next to him. "Sarah's not the only problem."

Louie's face reddened. "*You* don't understand. My room looks a mess, but I know where everything is."

"I don't like messes, organized or not. The family room looks like a landfill." Mom ran her fingers through her short brown hair. "You don't understand. I work all day at the office, clean a messy house at night, and I can't eat dinner in peace. I love Sarah, too, Louie, but something has to be done right away."

Mom looked tired, but determined.

"I'll help out, Mom. Sarah will listen, you'll see. She'll learn."

After cleaning his room and losing his homework, Louie read *Polite Pets* and taught Sarah to sit, stay, and roll over. Mom rewarded Sarah for her tricks with a Canine Candy dog treat. Sarah rewarded herself with a bag of barbecue-flavor potato chips that had been left on the table.

After picking up the family room and misplacing a library book, Louie called the vet. Dr. Domuch thought Sarah misbehaved because she needed more exercise.

Louie walked Sarah each morning, threw the ball to her after school, and played tug of war until he thought his arms or Sarah's teeth would give out. Tired from all the exercise, Louie fell into bed. Hungry from all the exercise, Sarah guzzled a bowl of salsa.

Mrs. Fishkeet at the pet shop suggested tricking Sarah. "Why don't you fill a hot dog bun with chili peppers and leave it out for her to steal? One mouthful and she'll never snatch anything from the counter again."

While Louie worried about late homework and an overdue book, he speared three green chilies with a fork and tucked them into the bun. A little of the juice dripped on his hand. He touched his fingertips to his tongue. It felt like molten lava in his mouth. He gulped three glasses of water.

Louie placed the chili-pepper bun on a plate. "This sure is a great lunch. I'll leave it on the counter while I look for last week's homework. I hope nothing happens to this tasty meal."

Sarah, curled in a tight "O" on the kitchen rug, lifted her head. Her wet nose quivered.

Louie left the lunch unguarded. It wasn't long before he heard clicking nails pausing to investigate, an eager snuffling, and a plate scraping against the counter.

He rushed to the kitchen. "I'm sorry, girl. I want you to understand . . . "

Sarah stood on her hind legs, her front paws holding down the plate on the counter. She burrowed her nose into the bun, devoured the last chili, and burped. After settling on the rug, she fell into a contented sleep.

Sarah ate the peppers and left the bun, thought Louie. He considered Sarah's other thefts—the Chinese dinner, pepperoni pizza, hot dog, chips. Now he understood.

Louie called the Pets for Families Animal Shelter and spoke with the manager. She remembered Sarah and told Louie about Sarah's first home.

That evening the aroma of tacos greeted Mom. "You made dinner. Is there a special occasion?"

"I understand how much work it is taking care of Sarah and cleaning the house," said Louie, "and I wanted to help, but . . . "

"But what?"

Louie explained about the lost homework and overdue book. He couldn't find them in all the neatness. Mom agreed that he could keep his organized mess in his room, but not the family room.

After dinner, Louie fixed Sarah's dog food. In a few minutes, she emptied her bowl and curled up on the rug.

"Sarah ate her dog food. She didn't even try to steal my taco. This *is* a special occasion. How'd you do it?" asked Mom.

"How are Chow Chicken, salsa, and barbecue-flavor chips alike?"

Mom looked puzzled. "Sarah ate them last week?"

"And they're all spicy."

Louie explained about calling the shelter. "Sarah's real name is Serrano. Her first owner, Mrs. Martinez, is a cook. She fed Sarah regular dog food, but she always mixed in leftovers from the restaurant."

"Serrano? That sounds familiar," said Mom. "Where does Mrs. Martinez work?"

"Mexican Food Inn," said Louie.

"Now I remember. Serrano is a chili."

"Sarah likes spicy leftovers. She tried to tell us by snatching what she wanted."

Louie showed Mom the jar of peppers. "Although you wouldn't want to do this with just any dog, Sarah's special. A few bits of serrano chili and dog food are a recipe for a happy dog."

Mom scratched Sarah's ear. "And listening to each other and understanding are a recipe for a happy family."

How Do You Spell Piranha?

By Harriett Diller

On Saturday morning, Madeline Burke found a note in her cereal bowl along with the Toasty O's. It said:

Eleven poor animals on their last breath,
Eleven poor animals starving to death.

Madeline knew exactly who had written that note. She found her mother at the desk in the living room and waved the note at her. "Very funny, Mom."

"It wasn't meant to be funny," Mrs. Burke said. She wrote something on the note pad in front of her.

"Not another note, Mom," said Madeline.

Mrs. Burke nodded. "I've got to get the point across to you somehow. You have to remember to feed your pets, Madeline. And I heard about a new study on the radio this morning."

"Another study?" Madeline said. Every time her mother heard about a new study, things were about to change at the Burke house. The last study had said that everybody ought to eat more oat bran. Now oat bran was a part of the Burke family diet.

Mrs. Burke nodded. "This study says that many people remember what they read much better than what they hear." She passed another note to her daughter.

Roses are red, violets are blue,
You need to eat. Your pets do, too.

Madeline groaned. "Very catchy, Mom. I guess that study said that most people remember rhymes better, too."

"Exactly," said Mrs. Burke. "Really, Madeline. I don't know how you plan to be an animal keeper at the zoo someday. You can't even remember to feed the few pets you have now."

"That's different, Mom," said Madeline. "I wouldn't forget to feed lions or boa constrictors or parrots."

Mrs. Burke scribbled another note.
The principle is the same,
Whatever the animal's name.
Madeline read the note and shoved it into her jeans pocket. "I have an announcement to make. I am going to feed my cat."

Madeline went to the kitchen and opened the bag of cat food. She carried the food outside and dumped it into Timber's dish. The orange cat purred in anticipation and began eating his breakfast. Madeline stroked Timber's back. "You really are a good cat," she whispered. "I'm sorry I forget to feed you."

Timber purred again.

"You know, Timber," said Madeline, "if you roared like a lion instead of purring, I bet I'd remember to feed you all the time." That gave Madeline an idea. "Know what, Timber? I promise you'll have your dinner on time tonight."

Timber did have his dinner on time that night. All the other animals got their meals that day, too. Madeline had no trouble remembering now that she was the keeper of Dr. Madeline's Strange and Amazing Creatures Zoo and Aquarium.

"Mom," said Madeline when they were sitting in the living room later. "Timber really roared for his supper tonight."

Mrs. Burke glanced up from her newspaper. "I didn't hear anything."

"That's because you don't have Dr. Madeline's trained ears. I bet you didn't hear the parrot calling either."

"Parrot?" said Mrs. Burke. "What parrot?"

"You know him as Old Yeller," said Madeline.

"The canary? I don't understand."

"The parrot and the lion are easy compared to those two boa constrictors," Madeline continued. "They're so quiet they're easy to forget."

"Boa constrictors!" said Mrs. Burke from behind her paper. "Where would you hide two boa constrictors in this tiny house?"

Madeline laughed. "Come on, Mom. They're in their cage. I'm talking about Jekyll and Hyde."

Mrs. Burke dropped the newspaper into her lap. "Your chameleons!" She smiled. "Now I understand." A moment later a puzzled expression replaced the smile. "But Madeline, how did you remember to feed the goldfish?"

Madeline walked over to the desk and picked up a pencil. She jotted something on the note pad, then glanced up at her mother. "How do you spell *piranha*, Mom?"

"Piranha!" Mrs. Burke stared at her daughter. "I think it's P-I-R-A-N-H-A."

Madeline finished the note. "It's easy to remember feeding the goldfish, Mom. Know why?" Madeline read the note.

Feed your piranhas unless you want to be thinner,
'Cause piranhas get hungry if they don't eat their dinner.

Trusty

By M. Donnaleen Howitt

Pete wished he wasn't afraid of dogs. He would like to have a dog like Lassie or the ones in books. Some of his friends said, "My dog won't hurt you. He never bites *me!*" Frankie's dog growled and snarled every time he saw Pete, and Chris's dog barked and showed its teeth even before Pete got near the door.

"Maybe the dogs sense that you are afraid of them," said Mom. "Try acting friendly and happy when you see them."

Pete tried with Mrs. Filmore's dog, Biscuit. It was a small dog that couldn't even reach the top of the fence.

"Nice doggie, good doggie," Pete called, smiling and trying to sound cheerful. From the other side of the fence, Biscuit followed Pete down the sidewalk. Just as they reached the end of the fence, Biscuit threw himself as hard as he could against the gate. Pete jumped back, startled, and a small shriek escaped his lips. That started Biscuit barking so loudly Mrs. Filmore came out to look. Pete hurried down the street, sure she was thinking he had teased Biscuit.

Pete's brother, Jeff, knew he was afraid of dogs. Sometimes Jeff teased him about the big black dog on Welton Street. When Pete passed by, that dog put its paws on the top of the chain link fence and barked as though a thief were in the yard. Pete always went blocks out of his way to avoid going near that dog.

One day, on the way home from school, Pete saw a dog ahead of him on the sidewalk. He slowed down, hoping the dog would turn the corner. Loose dogs could be dangerous. The dog moved very slowly. It was brown and shaggy— an in-between-sized dog—and it seemed to be limping. Pete crossed the street. He kept his eye on the dog and saw it was looking over at him. The dog stopped, held up one paw, and whimpered.

Pete started to move ahead. The dog whined, looking sad and lonely. Pete's heart thumped. He wanted to help, but he was afraid. He decided to cross over to the dog. If it growled, he could run, and the dog couldn't move very fast. The dog was lying down, resting its head on one paw. Pete moved closer and the dog looked up at him. It had nice brown eyes. Pete was still afraid. Sick and wounded animals might bite, thinking they would be hurt again. Pete took a deep breath and said, "What's wrong, boy?" Something moved, and Pete jumped back. Then he noticed that the movement was the dog's shaggy tail, thumping against the sidewalk.

Pete started to leave, and the dog whimpered. Pete looked back. The dog was sitting up. "I'll be back, boy, I promise," called Pete.

At the corner, Pete looked back again. The dog was following him, holding up one paw! Pete sighed and walked back to the dog. The tail swished again, and he could see that the paw was bleeding. Pete knelt beside the dog. The dog inched closer and laid its head against Pete's thigh. Pete dared to touch the dog's head. The fur was matted and dirty, but the tail swished again.

Pete lowered himself and sat down, the dog's head in his lap. *What'll I do?* Pete thought. *If I move, he'll follow and make that paw worse. I'm afraid to lift him. He might bite.*

Pete heard his name called and saw Jeff coming down the sidewalk. "Hey, Pete," he called. "What happened? Is that a *dog?* Won't he let you up?" Jeff was laughing. When he got closer, Pete explained.

"Stay here," said Jeff. "I'll go get the wagon. We can take him to the vet."

Pete talked softly to the dog while he watched for Jeff. He was surprised when Jeff and Mom pulled up in the car. "You boys put the dog on that old blanket in the back seat," said Mom. The dog didn't fuss, and Pete sat beside him on the way to the vet.

Doc Jensen took the dog into a back room. At last he came out, without the dog. "I'll keep him for a few days. He's in bad shape and needs rest. I gave him a shot." He turned to Pete and asked, "Did you find him? Want to say 'good-bye'?"

In the back room the dog lay on a table, a bandage around its paw. As Pete came near, the tail thumped madly. Doc Jensen said, "The way he looks at you, I think he feels better already. Maybe you've got yourself a dog."

On the way home, Pete checked with Mom. "Is there a chance we could keep him, Mom?"

Mom looked at him and smiled. "I'm so proud of you, Pete. I know it was hard for you to help that poor dog. And if he has no home, I think we should keep him."

"What'll we call him?" asked Jeff.

Pete smiled. "I think I'll call him . . . Trusty!"

"What kind of name is that?"

"Well," Pete explained, "he trusted me, and I trusted him . . . so that's his name . . . Trusty!"

"Guess you can call him anything you like," said Jeff. "He's *your* dog."

Pete leaned back and thought about what Jeff had said. He smiled and decided those were the nicest words he had ever heard.

Goldie's Rescue

By Genna White

When Meg got a kitten for her birthday, she took one look at the cat's gold eyes and yellow fur and said, "I'll call her Goldie."

Goldie became a member of the family in no time at all.

Meg rolled a ball on the floor, and Goldie batted it with her small paw.

Meg's brother Brett trailed a ribbon down the hall. Goldie chased after it.

Meg's mother scratched Goldie under her chin. Goldie purred and closed her eyes.

Everybody in Meg's family loved Goldie.

Everybody, that is, but Lucas.

Lucas was Meg's oldest brother, and he didn't seem to like Goldie one bit. Every day Meg watched to see if Lucas petted Goldie or played with her. But Lucas never did.

Sometimes Goldie wound around Lucas's legs at the kitchen counter. But Lucas just stepped away.

"Move, Goldie," Lucas said. "I'm making a sandwich. I don't have time to play with you."

A few times, Meg saw Goldie rub against Lucas's arm while Lucas sat on the floor doing his homework. But Lucas pushed Goldie aside.

"You're wrinkling my papers, Goldie," Lucas said. "Go find somewhere else to play."

One evening, Goldie crawled into Lucas's lap while he watched television. But Meg saw Lucas pick up Goldie and put her down on the floor.

"You can't sit in my lap, Goldie," Lucas said. "I don't want your fur all over me."

Meg wanted Lucas to like Goldie. But as the days passed, Meg started to give up hope.

"It's not your fault, Goldie," Meg said, scratching the kitten behind her ears. "Mom says Lucas has never liked cats. It's not just you."

Then one day Goldie went outside and didn't come back home.

Meg and Brett walked around the neighborhood, calling for her.

But they couldn't find her.

"Don't worry, Meg," Brett said when they got back to their own yard. "Goldie will come home."

Suddenly, Meg heard a noise.

"Be quiet," she whispered, putting her finger to her lips.

The noise came again. A soft *meow*.

"It's Goldie!" Brett cried.

Meg pointed to the branches of the big oak tree in their backyard. "I think she's up there."

Meg and Brett stood under the tree and peered up into the branches. A small yellow ball of fur crouched on one of the highest limbs.

"Goldie?" Meg called.

There was another *meow*.

"I'll climb up and get her," Meg said.

But she couldn't reach the lowest branch on the tree. Brett couldn't reach it either, not even when he jumped.

"Try to pick me up, Brett," Meg said. "Maybe then I can grab hold of the limb."

But Brett couldn't lift Meg more than a few inches off the ground.

"You're too heavy," he groaned.

"You don't have any muscles," Meg said.

They glared at each other for a minute. Then they both looked up into the tree again. Goldie didn't move.

The back door opened and Lucas came out of the house. Meg had an idea.

"I'll bet that Lucas could rescue Goldie," Meg said to Brett.

"But Lucas never even holds Goldie."

"Well, he has to hold her this time," Meg said. "Goldie's in trouble."

They called Lucas over and told him about Goldie. Lucas squinted up at the tree.

"Silly cat," Lucas mumbled.

For a few seconds, Meg was afraid that Lucas wasn't going to help them. But Lucas jumped into the air, grabbed hold of the lowest branch, and pulled himself up into the oak tree. He climbed higher and higher, until he finally reached Goldie.

Then Lucas tucked Goldie under his arm and climbed back down the tree.

"Here's the scaredy-cat," Lucas said, handing Goldie to Meg.

Meg buried her nose in the kitten's yellow fur.

"Thanks, Lucas," Meg said. "Do you think you could like Goldie now? Even a little bit?"

"Don't count on it," Lucas said. But he was smiling, too.

After that day, Meg watched to see if Lucas petted Goldie or played with her. At first, Lucas still acted as though he didn't like Goldie.

But one day, Meg saw Lucas slip Goldie something to eat.

Then Meg caught a glimpse of Lucas stroking Goldie's fur while he did his homework.

And sometimes, Lucas let Goldie sit in his lap while he watched TV—but only when Lucas didn't know Meg was watching.

Gary's Gecko

By Virginia L. Kroll

"Are we almost there? Are we almost there?" asked Amy for the hundredth time.

Gary saw Mama sigh. "Amy," he answered his sister, "we'll tell you when we get there. How about a story?"

"Yippee!" said Amy, handing her brother a book. He read *Frosty the Snowman* for the third time that day.

"There won't be any snowmen where we're going," Gary said when the story was finished.

"No snowmen?" Amy said sadly. "Then let's go home, Daddy."

"But it'll always be warm, and there will be pretty cactuses and lots of rocks and sand to play in. In fact, our new front yard is like a giant sandbox," Gary said, rekindling Amy's interest.

"Yippee!" Amy repeated her favorite new word.

After Gary's family stopped for a late supper, Mama took over driving for the last stretch of the trip. By the time they pulled into their new driveway in New Mexico, Amy had been sound asleep for an hour. "It's a long way from New York," Dad sighed.

"I'll help with the sleeping bags," Gary offered, too tired to think of exploring. Dad carried Amy in, and they all bedded down in the empty living room.

The sound of the moving van awakened them. Slightly refreshed from their exhausting trip, they got up and went right to work. At nighttime, Mama sank into the familiar couch and whistled, "Whew! What a day!"

"I'll say," agreed Gary, who had done his share of the unpacking.

"Relaxing never felt so good," said Dad, stretching out his legs.

Amy came out of her bedroom, rubbing her eyes. "There's something crawling on my ceiling," she whined, "with claws and shiny eyes and a long tail. And it squeaks."

"Amy, sweetheart, you're probably just having a bad dream from all this excitement. Come on, I'll take you back to bed," Mama offered. She picked up her drowsy child and headed for her bedroom down the hall.

A shriek resounded from Amy's bedroom, and Mama reappeared in a flash, clinging tightly to Amy. "John, she's right. There is something on her ceiling. Come quick!" Mama said to Dad, whose protective instinct had propelled him forward before Mama had even finished her sentence. Gary was right on his heels.

"There it is. I see it," Dad said as the creature began to move.

"John, get it, quick!" Mama yelled. "It's going down the wall."

"Oh Mama, it's only a gecko," Gary said.

"What's a gecko?" Amy asked, wide awake.

"It's a little lizard," Gary started to explain, but Mama's voice drowned him out.

"Get it, John, *right now*—before it gets away!" she shrieked.

The lizard moved its scaly tail from side to side. Dad reached out and *zap!* he grabbed it. "Gotcha!" he said. The lizard scampered back up onto the ceiling as Dad stood, dumb struck, holding the tip of its tail in his hand.

Gary laughed. "I'll take it outside." He stood on Amy's dresser and gently plucked the frightened lizard from the ceiling. He left Amy's room. Instead of going outside, however, he changed his mind and detoured to his own room.

"There. Now stay put," Gary warned the gecko. He closed his door and rejoined his family, who were beginning to recover from shock.

"Isn't that a great defense, losing your tail when somebody grabs you? A lot of lizards do that," Gary explained.

"It *was* quite a surprise," Dad said.

"I never saw such a thing in my life," Mama exclaimed with a shudder.

"Do geckos bite?" Amy asked sleepily.

"Not unless you're an insect, Amy. They don't bother people at all," Gary answered.

"Then I'm going back to bed," said Amy, jumping in and grasping her tattered elephant snugly. "I'm not afraid of a little lizard. Good night."

"Well I am," Mama whispered in the hall outside Amy's room.

"You'll get over it, Mama," Gary said, amused.

"I'm not fond of them, either, but I guess we'll have to get used to them," said Dad.

Gary's gecko came and went through the small opening that Gary fixed for it in his sliding screen. One morning at breakfast, Mama said, "I don't know if I'll ever get used to it here. The warm weather is nice, but oh, the things that go along with it! Last night I was up three times to kill insects that were buzzing around my head. I think I'd rather have lizards than bugs."

Gary smiled. Mama was mellowing already.

"I killed two insects last night myself," added Dad.

"I just pull my sheet over my head when I hear them," said Amy.

"Don't the bugs bother you, Gary?" asked Dad.

Gary smiled. "Never," he said knowingly.

Mama said, "I love this house. I'm getting used to the landscape, and I've met some fine people. You know how I feel about spraying pesticides; that's out of the question. I just wish there were something we could do about those bugs!"

"Actually," Gary began slyly, "there *is* something else."

He had just noticed the two hard-shelled gecko eggs hidden safely under the rock outside his bedroom window. His parents would be glad to have the little geckos when Gary explained how they would keep down the bugs.

SPOOKY
and the
DUCHESS

By Helen Kronberg

"I wish we could keep Princess," said Gina.

Aunt Lorna smiled. "Thank you for taking her. Princess would have been unhappy in a kennel for a whole month because she's such a peppy one. And now, Duchess may be glad for a rest." Aunt Lorna opened her car door, and Princess eagerly leaped inside.

Gina put her arm around her own big collie, Duchess, then she waved good-bye as Aunt Lorna and Princess drove away.

Duchess took a nap in the sun. When Mother called Gina for lunch, Duchess tagged along after her. She napped in a corner of the kitchen. She wandered around the house. She whined at the door, and Gina let her out. In a moment, she was back. She took a drink of water, then wandered to the patio windows.

"You must need a walk," said Gina. They took a long walk. They played in the yard. At supper-time, Duchess ate then wandered around again.

"She's looking for Princess," said Gina.

Mother nodded. "I think you're right. But she'll catch on soon."

The next day Duchess was still restless. And by the third day she wasn't eating much.

Aunt Lorna brought Princess for a visit. For a couple of days Duchess was OK. Then she again lost interest in food. She lost her pep.

"Duchess is lonesome," Gina said. "Couldn't Aunt Lorna bring Princess to visit every day?"

"Aunt Lorna is too busy to come every day."

"Maybe we could get another dog," said Gina.

Mother laughed. "Come on, Gina. Duchess will adjust in time."

But Duchess didn't adjust. She quit wandering around, but she didn't eat much. Her coat began to lose its luster.

"We just have to get company for her," Gina said. "Please, Mom."

Mother sighed. "I really don't need two dogs."

"There are all kinds of great dogs at the animal shelter," Gina continued. "And they need homes."

"I guess you're right," her mother said. "It's worth a try."

At the shelter they looked at big dogs and little dogs, and old, young, and in-between dogs.

"There's a good-looking collie," Mother said. "She isn't as nice as Princess. But she'll probably do."

Gina had already walked past the collie. The dog she was looking at scooted away as soon as Gina came near. "He spooks easily," the attendant said. "I suspect he's had some bad experiences."

The dog was medium size. It was gray, tan, and even had spots of white and orange.

"Poor thing," said Gina.

"What in the world is it?" Mom asked.

The attendant laughed. "I'd say he comes from a long line of true mongrels."

"Can we get that one?" Gina asked.

"Look at him," Mother said. "He doesn't want anything to do with us."

"But he needs someone to love him. Probably nobody will take him. If we give him lots of love, maybe he wouldn't be so scared any more."

"She's right about that," said the attendant. "It's going to take patience. But the dog is young, and he's in excellent health."

"I think we should take the collie," said Mother.

"But, Mom . . ."

Mother sighed.

"Since you already have a collie, I'd be tempted to advise taking another one. But you could give this one a try. If it doesn't work out, bring him back. I'll hang onto the collie just in case," the attendant said.

"We'll give it two weeks. That should be time enough, shouldn't it?"

The attendant shook her head. "I really can't say. It's possible, I suppose, to see some change in a couple of weeks. Just don't expect a real big change overnight."

She spoke soothingly to the dog as she picked him up. Then, gently, she gave him to Gina.

The dog's little heart beat like a jackhammer. But he didn't try to get away.

Gina held him gently but firmly. When they got home, she put him on the floor beside Duchess. "We got you a friend," she said.

Duchess sniffed the new dog. Then she walked away. The new dog scurried into a corner of the kitchen, and sat with his tail between his legs.

"Poor Spooky," said Gina. She put a dog biscuit on the floor beside him.

"Spooky?"

"It fits," said Gina. "The attendant said he spooks easily. He hides in dark corners." She laughed. "I wonder if he comes out at night."

Duchess whined to go out. "Yeah, Duchess," Gina said. "Your friend should go out, too." She put a leash on Spooky.

Spooky didn't want to go at first. Gina gave him lots of time. She walked him around the yard. Often she stopped beside Duchess, hoping they would make friends. But Spooky was wary and Duchess ignored him.

At last she let Spooky explore the yard by himself. She played with Duchess. Then she climbed a tree to look out over the neighborhood.

Each day she worked on Spooky. In time he became less afraid of her. But he was still spooked by strangers or any loud noise. Duchess remained aloof.

Then one day the fire engine, sirens blaring, sped past the house. Spooky cowered in a corner of the yard. He whimpered, trembling so hard Gina thought he would fall apart.

Duchess loped over to him. She licked his face. She gave a gentle "woof" and snuggled closer. She nuzzled and nearly covered him with her huge, furry body. Soon they were playing.

Gina went into the house, careful not to slam the door. "It's working, Mom," she whispered. "Come and see."

Gina smiled. "Duchess needed someone to take care of," she said. "And Spooky needed someone to understand his fears."

She looked up at her mother. "I know Spooky isn't really cured yet. But we won't have to take him back, will we?"

"What? Take back a dog that needs us so much?" Mother said. "What would Duchess think?"

The Ostrich and the Clarinet

By Kathryn Lay

Brandon pushed past the two ostriches trying to stick their heads inside his backpack.

"Come on, stop it already," he said.

His mother glanced up from bandaging a cut on another ostrich's leg. "They're just being curious."

Brandon shrugged and plopped down on the back porch.

"They're always curious. Why are they always in the backyard?"

His mother stood and patted the brown ostrich on the tail feathers. "I just like spending time with the girls."

She sat beside Brandon. "What's wrong? Bad day at school?"

He nodded. "It's this dumb clarinet. I wish I had never signed up for band. Most elementary schools don't even have band, and my playing makes me sound like a sick elephant."

His mother patted the clarinet case. "The more you play, the better you'll sound."

"Practicing isn't any fun when you sound awful," Brandon explained.

"The male ostrich came today."

Brandon looked up. "Really? Where is he?"

"In the ostrich yard," his mother said, pointing to the large, fenced-in field. "He's a little shy and doesn't want to make friends yet."

Brandon jumped up and ran across the grass to the fence. Inside, the male ostrich strutted around the yard. He was black, not brown like the females, and he had long white feathers on his tail.

Ever since his parents had decided to start an ostrich farm, Brandon couldn't wait to get the male. They were huge. The book he'd read said they could weigh 300 pounds when they were full grown and grow eight feet tall.

He watched the ostrich pace the yard. This one was still young, only a little taller than Brandon. It stared at Brandon a moment, then walked to the other side of the yard.

Later, Brandon took his clarinet outside to practice. His baby sister cried whenever he played inside the house.

He wandered across the yard to the ostrich pen and climbed up on the wooden fence. For a while, he watched the huge birds and sucked on the reed of his clarinet as though it were an ice-cream stick. Then he tacked a piece of music to a post and began to play.

The instrument squawked and squeaked, not sounding much like the music he knew he should be playing.

He looked up at the new ostrich, who had stopped eating to stare at Brandon.

"It's supposed to be the 'Star Spangled Banner.' But I'm a horrible musician," he explained.

The ostrich cocked his head.

Brandon shrugged and played again. The ostrich took a few steps closer. Then a few more.

Brandon stopped playing. The ostrich stopped walking and looked at him.

Brandon put the clarinet to his lips again. He blew and the ostrich came closer. When it was just a few feet from the fence, it began moving its long neck from side to side. The big, two-toed feet pawed the ground.

"You look like you're dancing," Brandon said.

He played for an hour while the ostrich strutted and pranced in front of him.

The next week, Brandon practiced every day after school. He couldn't wait to come home and play his clarinet. Orville, the name he'd given the ostrich, never seemed to tire of dancing. He even let Brandon touch him.

At the end of the week, Mr. Helton, the band director, said Brandon's playing had improved faster than anyone else's.

That afternoon, Brandon hurried home to tell Orville. After all, he had never enjoyed practicing until the ostrich came.

He ran to the fence. The four females paced the ostrich yard, but Orville wasn't with them.

"Mom, where's Orville?" Brandon shouted, bursting into the kitchen.

His mother frowned. "When I came home from the feed store, the gate was open and the females were huddled in a corner. Your father and Uncle James are out searching for Orville."

Brandon bit his lip and stared at his mother. Orville was gone?

Once, one of Mr. Foster's goats from down the road had gotten loose and wandered into the hills. A coyote got her.

Brandon's father and uncle walked in the back door, slamming the screen behind them.

"We've looked everywhere. He could be hiding in those woods at the foot of the hills," Brandon's father said.

"I can find him," Brandon shouted. He grabbed his clarinet and ran outside, followed by his father and uncle.

"What are you up to, son?" his father asked.

"You'll see," Brandon said, jumping into the back of the old blue pickup.

"Drive slowly," he said as his father and uncle climbed inside the truck's cab.

They drove down the dirt road that led to a small forest of trees. Brandon sat on a bench in the truck and played his clarinet. He played "The Star Spangled Banner" as loud as he could.

An orange-red glow filled the sky as the sun sank behind the hills. Brandon knew that in the dark it would be hard to see the black ostrich.

He was beginning to run out of breath when he saw something tall and dark standing beside a rock. *Just a tree,* he thought.

The tree moved.

"There he is!" Brandon shouted, pounding on the side of the truck.

His father turned the truck around and stopped.

Brandon took a deep breath and played the clarinet again.

Orville walked over to the truck. He stuck his head inside and blinked at Uncle James. Then, he bobbed his head at Brandon as if to say, "Let's dance."

As Brandon played, his father drove the truck slowly home.

Orville danced along behind them.

When Orville was safely back inside the pen with the other ostriches, Brandon's father scratched his head and asked, "How did you do that?"

Brandon smiled and tucked the clarinet under his arm. "It was easy. It just took practice."

The Dog Lover

By Jean Doyle

Nora loved dogs of all kinds. She read every book she could find, watched every dog show on TV, collected stuffed dogs big and small, and even cut out dog pictures from old magazines. But Nora did not own a dog.

"It's not fair," she said for the hundredth time. "A real dog is the thing I want most of all."

"I know," sighed her mother for the hundredth time. "I wish you could have one. But you know it's not possible, at least for now."

"But it's still not fair," Nora repeated.

"No, it isn't," agreed her mother. "But neither is it fair that your little brother sneezes and has an allergic reaction whenever he is around dogs. You know how sick he can get."

Nora did know. Many times she had watched Sean's eyes get watery and his face start swelling when he was around dogs.

Nora's mother put an arm around her shoulder.

"Look, honey," she said as she saw the tears fill Nora's eyes. "Some day you will be able to have a dog—more than one if you want. Someday you will have a home of your own. Or maybe there will be a way for Sean to be free of his asthma attacks. But until then we can't have a dog in this family."

Nora gave her mother a hug in return. "I know," she said. "But a stuffed dog just isn't as good as a real one."

A week later Nora was walking to the grocery store for some milk. As she turned onto Market Street, she noticed a woman and her little dog coming toward her. She knew the dog was a poodle, a bouncy little reddish one. Nora thought it looked almost pink.

The woman smiled and Nora asked, "What's your dog's name?" It wagged its short tail and tried to jump up on her.

"Down, Daphne," laughed the woman. "I guess she likes you. She doesn't usually greet people this way."

"I love dogs," Nora said, scratching the little dog's ears. "Maybe Daphne can sense that. I read that once in a dog book."

"I think you're right," agreed the woman. Then she added, "My name is Gail Adams. Daphne and I live in the apartment house on the corner."

Soon Nora was seeing Gail and Daphne several times a week as they walked down Hamilton Avenue together. Gail was very regular, so Nora knew the best times to meet them. The minute Daphne saw Nora she would begin jumping up and down in excitement.

"One of these days she's going to do a back-flip," laughed Gail.

When school was out for the summer vacation, Nora met the little apricot poodle and her mistress daily. But one day Gail had some disturbing news.

"An old sports injury is causing pain in my left foot, and I'll have to have surgery on it in a few days," she told Nora. "The doctor says I'll have a cast, and I must keep my leg propped up on a footstool. I'm afraid you won't be seeing Daphne and me for a couple of weeks. She'll have to stay in the kennel until my foot heals."

Nora's mother could see that Nora was very unhappy when she returned from her walk. "I'm sorry," she sympathized. "I know how fond you've grown of Daphne."

Suddenly Nora had an idea. Her mother quickly agreed when she told her about it.

Nora raced all the way to Gail's apartment. When she explained her plan, Gail smiled and gave her a hug.

"That will be so much better than putting Daphne in the kennel for three weeks," she agreed. "And I will insist on paying you for helping me."

When Nora started to protest, Gail said, "It's the only way I'll agree to it."

So it was settled. Every day at 8:00 in the morning, at noon, at 3:00 in the afternoon, and in the early evening Nora came to get Daphne and take her for a long walk. They walked to the park, to the schoolyard, to the ball field, and sometimes just around two long blocks. It was hard to tell who was happier—Nora or Daphne.

All too soon three weeks had passed, and Nora took Daphne for their last walk together. "I'm sure going to miss playing with you," she told the little poodle. "It was almost like you were my own dog." Daphne's wagging tail seemed to show she agreed.

Gail handed Nora an envelope with fifty dollars in it. When Nora started to say it was too much, she said, "You were a bargain. Daphne seems very fond of you, and we'll still see you when we go for our walks."

As she took the elevator down to the ground floor, Nora couldn't help thinking, "Now I'm without a dog again. It sure was fun pretending Daphne was mine."

She opened the big apartment building door and nearly bumped into two women. "Oh," said the tall one, "I believe you're just the person we want to see."

The shorter woman added, "We were talking to Gail Adams, and she told us what a good dog walker you are. Would you be able to walk my Freddie three times a day? He is very agreeable and I know he wouldn't give you any trouble. I'll pay you, of course."

"And I'm going to start doing some volunteer work at the hospital," said the tall woman. "My Beatrix will need to be walked, too. Could you take both dogs at the same time?"

Nora couldn't believe her good luck. "Yes, yes, I think so," she stammered.

When Nora told her mother, she said, "Nora's Dog-Walking Service sounds wonderful. You have proven yourself responsible with Daphne, so I know you can handle two more dogs."

For the rest of the summer Nora joined Gail four times a day, walking Daphne the poodle, Freddie the bulldog, and Beatrix the spaniel. And when school started up again, Nora found she still had time to walk Freddie and Beatrix in the morning and evening.

"I guess there's more than one way to have a dog," she told her mother.

A Friend for Tillie

By Judy Cox

"Hi, Tillie," whispered Juan. He crouched beside the cage and gently scratched the prairie dog behind her ears. There was a bare patch of skin across the bridge of her nose. It bothered Juan. He hoped she wasn't sick.

Before coming to Huddleston School, Juan had never even seen a prairie dog. His old school didn't have pets. Huddleston had five: a python, a rat, a goldfish, a hedgehog, and Tillie. Tillie was Juan's favorite. Every day, he stopped by her cage. He thought Tillie liked him, too, because she always waddled out of her cardboard house to see him.

The bell rang. Juan reluctantly told Tillie good-bye and headed off to class.

Mr. Millson was talking when Juan slid into his seat. He was reminding them that the animal projects were due next month. Juan already knew what animal he wanted to study. Prairie dogs!

After lunch, Juan headed for the library. He didn't mind missing recess. Since he was new, he didn't have anyone to play with anyway. Give it time, Mom kept saying. He didn't care. He liked the quiet of the empty library.

To his surprise, there was another kid from his class there. He thought her name was Glenna. She sat at a table, reading, her glasses slipping down over her nose. She pushed her glasses up with her index finger when she saw him. "Hi!" she called.

Juan didn't know what to do, so he ignored her, and went to the section of the library where they kept the animal books. He searched the shelves for books on prairie dogs.

"What animal are you doing?" Glenna whispered.

"Prairie dogs."

"I don't know what I'm going to do," she moaned, pushing her glasses up on her nose. "I haven't even started, and I can't think of anything. Why'd you pick prairie dogs?"

Juan found a book and checked it out. Glenna followed. Out in the hall, he turned to her. "Prairie dogs are cool," he said. "And I really like Tillie. But did you ever notice that she has this bare patch of skin on her nose, like she's been rubbing it on her cage? I don't know why. But I'm going to try to find out." Juan and Glenna walked down the hall to Tillie's cage. Tillie stopped nibbling her pellets when she saw them and waddled over to sniff Juan's fingers.

"Won't she bite?" asked Glenna.

Juan shook his head. "She likes to be scratched. Come on, you try." Glenna gingerly held out her fingers. Tillie sniffed them and rubbed her chin against them.

"Hey!" said Glenna. "I'll do my project on prairie dogs, too! We'll work together. That's more fun than working alone." She pushed her glasses up and smiled. Juan didn't know what to say. He hadn't counted on a partner, and a girl at that. But maybe she was right. Maybe it would be more fun with someone else. Finally, he smiled back.

Every day after lunch, Juan and Glenna met to work on prairie dogs. Besides a report, they had to do a project. They took notes and typed their report on the class computer. But they couldn't decide on a project.

And Juan still hadn't found out why Tillie was rubbing the fur off her nose.

"Listen to this," he told Glenna one day. They sat in the hall next to Tillie's cage, a stack of books beside them. "It says here prairie dogs are social animals. They live together in prairie dog towns." He looked thoughtfully at Tillie, curled up in her cage. "Do you think she's lonesome?"

Glenna pushed her glasses up. "Maybe that's why she keeps rubbing her nose on the bars. Maybe it's a nervous habit. Like scratching!"

Juan stood up. "I'll bet that's it. I'll bet she's lonesome. In the wild, prairie dogs live with other prairie dogs. She needs a friend."

The next day, Juan called the pet store. "Another prairie dog would cost $100," he told Glenna. "I don't have that kind of money. But I have an idea. This can be our project for Mr. Millson's class! We'll raise money to buy another prairie dog."

"How?"

"Lots of ways. Collect pop cans. Have a car wash. Have a raffle. Hold a bake sale."

"Yeah! And we can get other classes to help, too."

The next few days, Juan and Glenna went to each classroom and made a presentation. "Prairie dogs are friendly," Juan told the kindergarten. "They greet each other by touching front teeth. It looks like kissing." The kindergarteners giggled.

"They live in towns," Glenna told the fifth grade. "They communicate by barking. We want to buy Tillie a friend to keep her company."

Donations of pop cans poured in from every class. Glenna and Juan sorted and washed hundreds of cans. Mr. Millson drove them to the store to return the cans and collect the deposit. Before long they'd made $100.

After school, they went to the pet store to buy a prairie dog. They picked out a young female.

The next day, they put the new prairie dog in Tillie's cage. The prairie dogs touched noses and sniffed each other. Tillie wriggled. "Look, she's happy," said Juan. He put his fingers in the cage and Tillie rubbed against him. "I think she's saying thank you."

"What are we going to name the new one?" asked Glenna.

Juan turned pink. He wanted to call the new prairie dog Glenna, after his first friend at Huddleston School, but he was too embarrassed to tell her. "How about 'Amigo'?" he said. "In Spanish, it means 'friend.'"

"Amigo," said Glenna. "I like it!"

Charlie

By Margaret Springer

Visiting hours were over. Lyndie followed Mom out of the hospital.

"Are you sure Dad will be OK?" she asked again, buttoning her coat against the wind as they headed across the parking lot.

"Yes, Lyndie," Mom said. "Dr. Cramer says his condition is serious but stable. He'll be home in a few days."

Lyndie hardly noticed the traffic as they drove home. She was remembering the sound of Dad wheezing and gasping in the middle of the night, and Mom's voice, desperate and scared, phoning for an ambulance.

Dad had had asthma before, but not like that.

At home Lyndie flopped onto the sofa and reached to pet Charlie, calmed as always by the feel of his thick, black fur. That was Dad's idea, to name the cat Charlie.

Charlie stretched, yawned, and hopped purring onto Lyndie's lap.

"That reminds me," said Mom. "We'll have to do something about Charlie. Dr. Cramer keeps mentioning it."

Lyndie looked up. "What?"

"He said it'll be better for Dad's allergies if there isn't a cat around when he gets home."

"When did he say that?" Lyndie's heart pounded. "Where can Charlie go?"

"I know it's hard." Mom gave her a hug, and sighed. "We'll ask around. I'm sure someone will be glad to give him a new home."

Lyndie felt her stomach tighten. "But he's not a kitten, Mom. He's an old cat. A sleepy old cat."

"Lyndie, I've talked to Dad about this. If we have to, the Humane Society—"

"No! It's not Charlie's fault! Charlie is the nicest cat in the whole world."

Charlie jumped off Lyndie's lap and disappeared under the sofa.

"We'll find a good home for him, Lyndie. Maybe Grandma can take him. And we can have another kind of pet."

"I don't want another pet. I want Charlie!"

Lyndie ran to her room.

The next day, she asked all her friends, all her teachers, all her neighbors, and anyone else she knew if they wanted a cat.

Nobody did.

Grandma said she'd like to, but she could not have pets at her apartment. Aunt Doris said she was sorry, but her dogs hated cats. Uncle Mo explained that Aunt Laura was allergic, too.

Everyone asked how Dad was.

Lyndie and Mom put notices in supermarkets and corner stores. They asked around at the hospital.

Nobody wanted a big, sleepy old cat.

On Thursday, Lyndie and Mom went to visit Great-grandma at the nursing home. Great-grandma was almost blind, and she didn't smile much, but she always stroked Lyndie's hair.

This week the residents were having a special music program. Some nodded and smiled and clapped. Many were in wheelchairs. Some just stared into space, mumbling.

It all seemed drab and depressing. Lyndie had seen sick people at the hospital all week, and now she was surrounded by these old people who needed to be cared for.

After the program Lyndie hung back. Great-grandma reached out and stroked her arm. Lyndie smiled, but she felt miserable.

Dad would be home on Saturday, two days from now. But first, they had to take Charlie to the Humane Society. Dr. Cramer had insisted.

Lyndie knew, deep down, that it was the right thing to do. She just hoped someone would be there who needed Charlie. She tried not to think of the alternative.

Outside it was almost dark, and a few snowflakes swirled in the frosty air. Lyndie and Mom were halfway to the car when Lyndie suddenly stood quite still for a moment. Then she turned and ran back toward the nursing home.

"Did you forget something?" asked Mom.

"No," Lyndie said, "but I have an idea."

She told Mom about it later.

Lyndie cried herself to sleep the first night after Charlie left. It took a lot of cleaning and vacuuming to make the house ready for Dad. Cat hairs were everywhere. But it was wonderful to have Dad home again.

The following Thursday Mom and Lyndie headed as usual for Great-grandma's. Lyndie felt tense and anxious. Her hands were tight fists in her lap.

The nursing home was brightly lit. It was more colorful than Lyndie remembered. Wonderful smells came from the kitchen. Lyndie felt her heart thump as she hurried into the main lounge.

"There he is!" she shouted.

There was Charlie, curled on a resident's lap, sleepily enjoying being stroked and smiled at and talked to.

"That was a great idea," Mom said.

"He's so popular already, they have to take turns," said a nurse. "Your Great-grandma hardly ever smiled before, but Charlie's working wonders. He's perfect. Charlie is the nicest gift we've ever had."

Lyndie sighed. A long, relieved, satisfied sigh. "He's the nicest cat in the whole world," she said. "And I will come and visit him every week."

Charlie looked up at Lyndie and yawned. She knew he understood every word.

The Pet Show

By Margaret Springer

At the time, I thought it was a great idea for a boring summer day.

"The Humane Society needs money for a new shelter," I said. "A pet show will be a good fund raiser. We'll charge fifty cents to enter."

"OK," my friend Angie said. "We'll have all kinds of pets. Even you, Izzy."

"I'm telling, I'm telling," Izzy said.

Izzy is my parakeet. Those are the only words he knows.

Mom said we could use the side yard. We live on a farm, so there's lots of space there.

We made registration forms and signs. We borrowed my brother Jason's markers.

"I'm telling, I'm telling," Izzy said.

Pet Show. All pets welcome, we wrote. *Must have cage or leash.*

We put the signs up around town.

"Maybe Mr. Holtz at the pet store will give us prizes," I said.

"Success should not be measured by the failure of others," Angie said. Angie's mother is a psychologist.

"OK," I said. "Everyone gets a ribbon."

Mr. Holtz agreed to be the judge and decide who gets which ribbon.

The day of the pet show was hot, hazy, and humid. Pets started arriving before we'd even finished breakfast.

There were dogs and cats, of course, in all shapes, sizes, and colors. Also Tweets the budgie. Joey the ferret. Sharlene the goose. Three rabbits. A pig. Hamsters and gerbils. They barked and meowed and snuffled and squeaked and squawked and grunted and chirped into our yard.

My brother Jason brought out Benjamina and Pinky in a box. Benjamina is a fig plant, and Pinky is an African violet.

"The form said all pets welcome," he said. "They're alive. I look after them."

"We'd better not hurt his feelings," Angie said.

He paid his fifty cents for each, so we started another category: planted pets.

My little sister Lisbeth carried something in grimy hands. "Here's Ervin the earthworm," she said.

"I'm telling, I'm telling," sang out Izzy.

For once Izzy was right. *No wild creatures captured to keep as pets*, our rules said. Lisbeth put Ervin back in the garden.

The air was thick and humid. Dark clouds hung on the horizon.

Sweat dripped down Mr. Holtz's back as he judged every entry.

The biggest pet, Ranger the sheep dog. The fluffiest, Pushkin the cat. The brightest eyes, Tweets. The shiniest coat, Joey. The longest neck, Sharlene. Soon every pet had a ribbon, even the planted ones. Benjamina was the quietest pet. Pinky was the most colorful.

Izzy, of course, was the most talkative.

A car pulled into our lane. It was Mr. Vetrocic, the photographer for the *Weekly Observer*. "I was just passing by," he said. "What a great shot!"

He lined everyone up. Just for the photo, some kids took their pets out of cages.

Everyone was careful. Everyone held on tightly to leashes.

Nothing would have happened if the sky hadn't chosen that moment to open.

Rain pelted down.

Pushkin the cat hates water. She screeched, claws out, and leaped out of her owner's arms.

Tweets the budgie thought Pushkin was after her and flew off into the bushes. Other cats took off after Tweets. Ranger and other dogs, pulling their owners by their leashes, took off after the cats.

Izzy rocketed out of my arms and flew over the whole commotion, squawking happily, "I'm telling, I'm telling."

Joey the ferret sprinted for cover under our back porch. Sharlene the goose honked and rushed up and down, flapping her wings. Rabbits raced crazily in every direction. The pig ran squealing into Dad's cornfield.

"This is a traumatic situation!" Angie shouted.

Rain poured down in buckets.

Angie and Mr. Holtz and Dad and I ran around trying to help catch them all. Mr. Vetrocic ran around taking pictures.

Mom called the Humane Society.

We found Pushkin hiding under the hedge. Tweets, her little heart thumping, flew back to her cage on her own. Joey and Sharlene and the rabbits were still at large. Dad helped us catch the pig, even though it meant trampling his corn.

By the time the Humane Society worker arrived, the downpour was about over. She helped us round up the last of the escapees. Soon, drenched, soggy owners were back in control and ready for home. Drenched, soggy pets were back on their leashes or secure inside cages.

All except Izzy.

"That bird will come down on his own," the worker said. "Parakeets are stubborn sometimes."

"I'm telling, I'm telling," Izzy sang out from a tree branch high above us.

I counted the money and gave it to the woman. My hands were scratched, my knees were muddy, and the money was soaking wet.

"Eleven dollars and forty-nine cents," I said. "We lost a penny somewhere."

"Thank you," she said. She had a funny smile on her face.

"Next summer, we'll definitely do better," Angie assured her.

"No." I looked at Angie and smiled. "Success is not measured by past failures."

Mr. Vetrocic was writing in his notebook. "Next time you kids have a good fund raising idea," he said, shaking rainwater out of his hair, "let me know about it ahead of time."

"I already have a good idea," I said.

My family looked worried.

"We'll have an art pet show, with *pictures* of pets," I said. "That will be a great idea for a boring summer day."

"But it won't be half as much fun," Angie giggled.

A SHORTCUT TO TROUBLE

By Marilyn Kratz

"I'm getting up, Mom," said Cassie, for the third time. She rolled over and pulled the blanket over her head.

Suddenly, she sat up.

"Oh, no!" she exclaimed. "I can't oversleep today!"

Cassie jumped out of bed, ran to the kitchen, and reached for a box of cereal.

"Aren't you going to get dressed before breakfast, dear?" asked Mom.

"I forgot!" Cassie started to run back to her room, but Mom stopped her.

"Slow down, Cassie," said Mom. "You'll meet yourself coming around a corner."

"But I can't be late for school today," said Cassie. My class is going on a field trip to the museum first thing this morning. If I'm late, I'll miss the bus that's coming to the school to pick us up."

"Why didn't you set your alarm clock to wake you?" asked Mom.

"I did," Cassie admitted, "but I was just too tired to get up when it rang."

"Why—" Mom began.

"Gotta run, Mom," Cassie interrupted as she rushed out of the kitchen. She didn't want to admit she'd watched TV in her room past her bedtime again last night. Besides, she was sure she could make up the lost time by hurrying—just as she had done all those other mornings when she had overslept.

She was only five minutes behind schedule when she rushed out the door on her way to school.

I can gain time by taking the shortcut over the bridge, thought Cassie. She crossed the vacant lot behind her house and started over the old wooden bridge. The bridge spanned a shallow creek that edged the lot.

Cassie had taken only a few steps onto the bridge when she heard something. It sounded like a baby's cry coming from under the bridge.

She stopped and listened. The sound stopped.

I must have imagined it, she decided and started to go on. Then she heard it again, along with a distinct meow.

Cassie ran across the bridge, then down the bank beside it. She looked under the bridge. On a narrow ledge of bank between the creek and bridge supports was Muffin, a small white cat that belonged to Cassie's neighbor, Mrs. Hanson.

"Come here, Muffin," urged Cassie. "Just follow that ledge over to me. Hurry!"

The cat meowed again, but it did not come.

"Come on, Muffin. You know me," Cassie coaxed. "I don't have much time."

Still the wet and shivering cat did not come.

What should I do? Cassie wondered. She looked back at the cat. His eyes seemed to beg for help.

Cassie sighed. "OK, Muffin," she said. "You win. I wouldn't enjoy the field trip knowing I left you here. I'll get you out and then run to school."

Cassie set her book bag down on the creek bank and inched toward the cat.

"Now I see the problem," she said. "Your collar is stuck on these weeds. Hold still, Muffin."

Cassie tugged at the weeds tangled around the cat's collar.

"You really know how to get into a jam, don't you, pal?" she said. "I'll have to lift you to get you untangled." When she had finally freed him, she and the cat were both muddy.

"Oh, Muffin," she said. "I'll have to go back home and change. I'll never make it to school on time."

Cassie picked up her book bag with one hand, and, holding Muffin in her other arm, she plodded back the way she had come. As she pictured her classmates excitedly boarding the bus—without her—tears of frustration spilled down her cheeks. *If only I'd have had more time,* she thought.

"Cassie! What happened?" exclaimed Mom, as Cassie stepped into the kitchen, still carrying the muddy cat.

"I had to help Muffin," said Cassie. "He was caught on some weeds under the bridge, and now I'm all muddy, and I'll miss the bus for the field trip, and I don't know what to do." She burst into sobs.

For a moment, Mom just stood there. Then she said, "Rescuing Muffin was a kind thing to do. I'm proud of you, Cassie. Now, take Muffin home. Then, while you get cleaned up, I'll call your teacher and tell her that you'll be late."

"But they'll leave for the field trip before I can get to school," said Cassie. "What will I do there until they get back?"

"I'll ask your teacher about that, too," said Mom.

Cassie carried Muffin across the yard to Mrs. Hanson's house.

"It's all your fault, Muffin—" she said. "If you hadn't—" Then she stopped. She sighed and went on.

"No, Muffin, it's my fault," she admitted. "I always oversleep and then rush to get to school. From now on, it's early to bed, early to rise for me, and no more missed field trips."

Cassie rang Mrs. Hanson's doorbell. "And, as for you, Muffin," she added, with a laugh, "no more trips to that creek. We've both learned a lesson there!"

My Name
Is
Jo-Jo

By Linda White

"That's the one I want," I said, looking back at the other baby parakeets to be sure. The little bundles wobbled in their nests. Their wings flapped uselessly as they tried to balance.

"Their downy feathers are yellow now," Mr. Chips said. "Soon real feathers will grow. These babies will be blue, these green, and those yellow."

I looked back at the bird I had chosen. He had no feathers at all. "What color will he be?"

"He should be green," Mr. Chips answered.

"Good. I like green best."

"Are you sure that's the one you want?" my mother asked.

"Yes, he needs me." I looked down at the naked bird. He had just hatched, and his skin was an odd mix of pink and blue. There were big blue bulges where his eyes would be, and his head was much too big for his body. He was so pitiful, he might not find a home if I didn't take him.

"I'll keep him for you. In five weeks he can leave his mama. You come back for him then."

Time dragged. The cage was ready, but every day I changed the mirror, toys, and perches around. At night I lay awake wondering and worrying. What if my bird didn't get feathers? What if he was still so ugly?

Finally, the day came to get my parakeet. When we entered the shed (Mr. Chips called it an aviary) where the birds were, a terrible racket arose as birds flew everywhere. "You are a good judge of birds," Mr. Chips praised. "Yours is the prettiest I've had in a long time. Smart, too. Here he is. Ain't he a beaut?"

I peered into the small cage that Mr. Chips held. Indeed he was beautiful! His body was bright green and his face was the color of daffodils. I was thrilled! "He's gorgeous!" I said. All my worry was for nothing. "Will he be able to learn his name?"

"Oh, sure," Mr. Chips replied. "Give him a short name and repeat it over and over. Be patient though. It will take time."

"His name's Jo-Jo," I said.

"That's good. He'll learn that."

We took him home and put him in his cage. At first, Jo-Jo was nervous. I walked gently to his cage, whistled softly, and repeated "My name is Jo-Jo" over and over. I spent hours with him, and soon he hopped down to a perch near me and crept cautiously closer. After a few days, he flew toward me when I came. Soon, I trained him to stand on my finger. Next, I let him out of the cage.

Jo-Jo enjoyed being with people and flew around to see what everyone was doing. When Dad read the paper, Jo-Jo perched on his hand and nibbled the evening news. He tried other papers, too, and more than once I turned in homework with Jo-Jo's mark. When my sister and I played jacks, he flew down and scattered them, disrupting our game. Best of all, he liked the sound of running water. When Mom washed dishes, the water drew him like a magnet. He stood on her shoulder chirping lustily until she finished. At night, we put him back in his cage.

One morning he sat chirping at the mirror. "Hello, my name is Jo-Jo!" he squawked.

"Jo-Jo just said his name!" I yelled. That was the first of many things he learned. He rubbed my cheek, saying, "Give me sugar, give me sugar!" He pressed his beak to my lips, making a smacking sound. Admiring his reflection in the mirror, he whistled and said, "Jo-Jo's a pretty bird." He even learned to whistle a few tunes.

One January day, the wind blew the door open. Jo-Jo flew outside. The whole family ran after him, frantically searching for his bright green shape. He should have been easy to spot against the snow, but we couldn't find him. That night was the coldest of the year. Two feet of new snow fell. We knew a small tropical bird could not survive the bitter cold. Still we searched. We asked everyone we saw if they had seen our Jo-Jo. No one had even had a glimpse of him. We were brokenhearted.

Finally, we cleaned out his cage and put it in the garage.

Weeks later, Mom was at the grocery store. She saw Mrs. Kloxen, a friend who lived three blocks away. While they talked together in the check-out line, Mother told her of our loss.

"What color is he?" Mrs. Kloxen asked.

"He was green with a bright yellow face," Mom told her.

"Could his name be Jo-Jo?" Mrs. Kloxen asked.

"Yes, it was," Mom said. "How did you know?"

"He's at our house!" she said. "Two weeks ago he crashed into our window. We brought him inside, and he's been telling us 'My name is Jo-Jo' ever since, but we didn't know whose Jo-Jo he was."

When I got home from school that day, Jo-Jo's sunny yellow face greeted me. I was so surprised and happy to see him! He flew to my shoulder and rubbed my cheek as I heard of his rescue.

"Hello, my name is Jo-Jo," he chirped.

"Jo-Jo," I said, "I think it's time to learn your phone number."

Worth Keeping

By Mary Ann Kuta

The school bus growled to a stop. Marci stepped from the noisy bus into the brooding silence of a rural November afternoon. Gray woolen clouds muffled the sky.

Suddenly she spun around. "Where's Duke?" she wondered. A frown creased her forehead. Duke never failed to greet her at the bus stop after school.

Marci scuffed through drifts of fallen leaves. She looked on one side of the lane and then the other, calling her dog's name.

She remembered when Duke had skittered across the freshly scrubbed kitchen floor with his muddy paws. Mother shook her head and said, "That dog is more trouble than he's worth." Marci defended her pet at times like that. Despite his faults, that black fur ball was her friend, and friends are worth keeping.

"Mom," Marci called as she entered the white farmhouse. "Have you seen Duke?"

"No, dear." Mother looked up. "Not since noon. He was snoozing on the porch when I had lunch."

After changing into her grubby clothes, Marci started to search the farmyard for her dog. She prowled through the barn.

Duke's mingled ancestry had produced a dog the size and shape of a floor mop, small enough to squeeze into all kinds of hiding places.

Marci dropped down on the ground and peered into the dark space under the chicken coop. Yuck! *Bugs and spiders and probably mice under here, too*, she thought, *but no dog*. She stood up, brushing the dirt off her clothes.

The crunch of gravel announced a car pulling into the driveway. Marci dashed around the corner of the house.

"Dad," she yelled, yanking on the door handle. "Duke's gone."

Dad stepped from the car, looking tired as he always did after the long drive home. "Have you looked everywhere?"

Marci nodded. "Everywhere in the yard."

Dad patted her shoulder. "Don't worry. He'll be back for dinner and a warm bed."

But Duke didn't come back that evening. The next morning Marci could tell her parents were worried, too.

"After we get back from grocery shopping, we'll form a line and comb the fields," Dad said, zipping up his jacket.

Mom nodded in agreement. "Are you sure you won't come with us?"

Marci shook her head. Saturday morning in town was usually one of her favorite activities, but not today.

Marci waved good-bye from the porch. As soon as the car was out of sight, she headed quickly for the woodlot.

The ancient oaks creaked as she crunched beneath their lowering branches. She checked every shrub and pile of brush.

"Duke?" she called every few minutes.

When Marci emerged from the grove into the lane, she heard the faint *whup-whup* of passing semi trucks on Interstate 80, a mile away. Duke's short legs couldn't carry him that far, could they? She felt her eyes sting with sudden tears.

Bowing her head into the wind, Marci trudged down the lane to the crossroads. "Where are you?" she shouted. A rude gust of wind snatched the words from her mouth.

The wind blew harder, whipping her hair into tangles. She cut back through a harvested field, shuffling through the stubble. Dust blew into her half-shut eyes. Bits of grit stung her face like pin pricks. The wind moaned a high-pitched whine— or was that the wind?

"Duke?" She listened carefully. "Duke?" The whining seemed to come from the edge of the field. Marci raced across the rough, dry earth, stumbling over the deep furrows. Reaching the boundary fence, she pulled back the overhanging branches of a thornbush, weighted with scarlet rose hips.

There he was, his collar caught on a piece of fence wire as tightly as if she had tied him there. Duke was tired but unhurt, his fur so matted with seeds and stickers that he looked like a miniature haystack with black legs. Marci giggled.

She crouched down and struggled to pry the collar off the wire. In spite of his weariness, Duke wagged his tail and licked her arm.

She did it! Marci rocked back on her heels. Realizing he was free, her black mop exploded with joy. He raced away, circled back, and somersaulted at her feet.

Marci felt like doing a somersault herself. Instead, she patted Duke's bobbing head and smiled her widest smile.

Later, Marci sat on the porch steps removing stickers from her dog's fur. Duke wriggled into her lap. She lifted his matted ear. "I'm glad you're back, Duke," she whispered. "You sure do get in a lot of trouble, but you're a good friend—and definitely worth keeping."